Mrs Jol
Joke Shop

by ALLAN AHLBERG

with pictures by
COLIN McNAUGHTON

PUFFIN

PUFFIN BOOKS

Published by the Penguin Group
Penguin Books Ltd, 80 Strand, London, WC2R 0RL, England
Penguin Group (USA), Inc., 375 Hudson Street, New York, New York 10014, USA
Penguin Books Australia Ltd, 250 Camberwell Road, Camberwell, Victoria 3124, Australia
Penguin Books Canada Ltd, 10 Alcorn Avenue, Toronto, Ontario, Canada M4V 3B2
Penguin Books India (P) Ltd, 11 Community Centre, Panchsheel Park, New Delhi – 110 017, India
Penguin Group (NZ), cnr Airborne and Rosedale Roads, Albany, Auckland 1310, New Zealand
Penguin Books (South Africa) (Pty) Ltd, 24 Sturdee Avenue, Rosebank 2196, South Africa

Penguin Books Ltd, Registered Offices: 80 Strand. London WC2R 0RL, England

puffinbooks.com

First published 1988
038 - 38

Text copyright © Allan Ahlberg, 1988
Illustrations copyright © Colin McNaughton, 1988

Educational Advisory Editor: Brian Thompson

Manufactured in China
Filmset in Century Schoolbook (Linotron 202) by
Rowland Phototypesetting (London) Ltd.

British Library Cataloguing in Publication Data
A CIP catalogue record for this book is available from the British Library

ISBN: 978-0-14032-347-4

I say, I say, I say –
have you heard the story
of Mrs Jolly's joke shop?
No?
Well, here it is.

One morning Mrs Jolly sat up in bed.
She heard a knock at the door.
Knock, knock!
"Who's there?" said Mrs Jolly.
"Boo!" said a voice.
"Boo who?" said Mrs Jolly.
"There's no need to cry," said the voice.
"It's only a joke!"
And in came Mr Jolly with a cup of tea.
Mrs Jolly had a laugh.
She drank her tea
and came downstairs for breakfast.

In the kitchen she heard
a voice from under the table.
"What's bread?" said the voice.
"Raw toast!" said Mrs Jolly.
And out popped Jennifer Jolly
with a plate of toast and honey.

Mrs Jolly had another laugh.
She ate her toast and honey
and went upstairs to get dressed.

At nine o'clock Mrs Jolly
put on her funny nose
and her silly hat
and went to work in the joke shop.

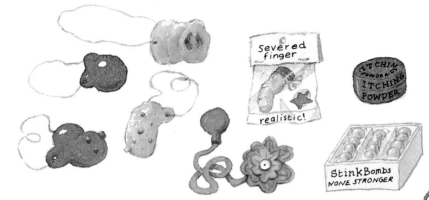

In Mrs Jolly's joke shop
there were lots of funny noses
and silly hats;
also lots of water-pistols,
water-flowers and water-rings.
There were squeaky cushions
and plastic spiders,
and lots and lots of jokes.

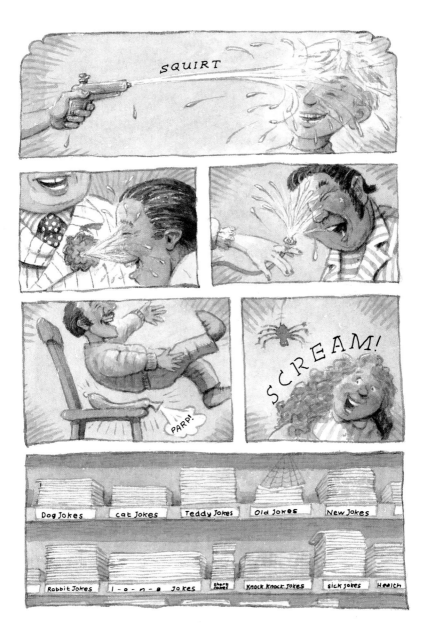

At ten past nine
the first customer came in.
He bought a funny nose,
a silly hat
and a joke about teddy bears.

A Jolly
Joke Card

Q. How do you start
a teddy bear race?

A. Ready, teddy, go!

At half-past nine
the second customer came in.
She bought a funny nose,
a silly hat
and a joke about rabbits.

A Jolly
Joke Card

Q. What do you get if you
pour boiling water
down a rabbit hole?

A. Hot cross bunnies!

At half-past ten
the window-cleaner came in –
straight through the window.
His ladder had broken.

At twelve o'clock Jennifer Jolly
came home for her lunch.
Mr and Mrs Jolly had theirs, too.
"What's white on the outside,
green on the inside and hops?"
said Jennifer.
And Mrs Jolly laughed and said,
"A frog sandwich!"

At half-past one Jennifer Jolly
went back to school
"Now, Jennifer," said her teacher.
"If I had five oranges in one hand,
and four in the other – what would I have?"
"Big hands, Miss!" said Jennifer.

At two o'clock Mr Jolly went shopping.
He went to a pet shop
to get a present for Mrs Jolly.
"I want a parrot for my wife," he said.
"Sorry, sir," said the pet-shop lady,
"we don't do swops."

At three o'clock a *robber*
came into Mrs Jolly's joke shop.
He pointed his finger at Mrs Jolly.
"This is a muck-up!" he said.
"Don't you mean a stick-up?"
said Mrs Jolly.
"No," said the robber. "A muck-up.
I forgot my gun!"
And out he went.

At four o'clock Jennifer Jolly
came home for her tea.
Mr and Mrs Jolly had theirs, too.
And the parrot had his.
"What's the best thing
to put into a pie?" said Mrs Jolly.
And the parrot said, "Your beak!"

At five o'clock it began to rain.
At six o'clock it was still raining,
and at seven,

and at half-past seven.
At eight o'clock the river bank broke
and the town was flooded.

The Jolly family climbed on to the roof.
"What goes up when the rain comes down?"
said Mr Jolly.
"An umbrella!" Mrs Jolly said.

At nine o'clock
there was a small earthquake
and the chimneys on the roof fell off.
"What did the big chimney
say to the little chimney?" said Jennifer.
"You're too young to smoke,"
Mr and Mrs Jolly said.

A few days later,
when the rain and floods had gone
and the house was clean again
and the window was mended,
Mrs Jolly put on her funny nose
and her silly hat
and went to work in the joke shop.

At five past nine
there was a knock at the door.
Knock, knock!
"Who's there?" said Mrs Jolly.
"Cows go!" said a voice.
"Cows go who?" said Mrs Jolly.
"No – cows go *moo*!" said the voice.
And in came the milkman.
Mrs Jolly laughed.
"Two pints, please!" she said.
And she went into the kitchen ...

... to make a pot of tea.

The End